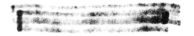

THE FISH IN OUR CLASS

Mitchell Lane
PUBLISHERS

Printing   1   2   3   4   5   6   7   8   9

The Fish in Our Class
The Frog in Our Class
The Hamster in Our Class
The Turtle in Our Class

Library of Congress Cataloging-in-Publication Data applied for

ISBN: 9781584159780
eBook ISBN: 9781612281476

ABOUT THE AUTHORS: Avid book reader and designer, Sharon L. Beck, has worked in the publishing business for over 20 years designing and laying out books, and learning all aspects of the publishing world. This is her first collaborated book. She lives in Delaware in her cozy little house with her fat, black cat, Miss Ellie. In her spare time she loves cooking, gardening, and spending time with family and friends.

First-grade teacher Jamie Lapsley earned her masters degree in elementary education from Wilmington University. Jamie saw the need for read-aloud books that relate to curriculum standards for pre-kindergarten and early elementary students. Since these books were often hard to come by, Jamie decided to develop her own collection, Little Jamie Books, for Mitchell Lane Publishers. She lives in Newark, Delaware, with her husband and their two puppies, Lily and Leroy.

PLB

CORNER

PET

THE FISH IN OUR CLASS

SHARON L. BECK &
JAMIE LAPSLEY

Mitchell Lane
PUBLISHERS
P.O. Box 196
Hockessin, Delaware 19707
Visit us on the web: www.mitchelllane.com

"Good morning," Miss Smith smiled at her class. "Today is going to be a very special day. I have new friends to introduce you to."

The entire class began to squirm in their seats with excitement.

As Katie eagerly raised and waved her hand, Miss Smith pointed to her. Katie asked, "Do we have new students?"

"Do we have special visitors?" Toby exclaimed.

"No and no," Miss Smith smiled. She looked over at her desk to the covered items.

"Oh! We have a new class pet!" several students cried out.

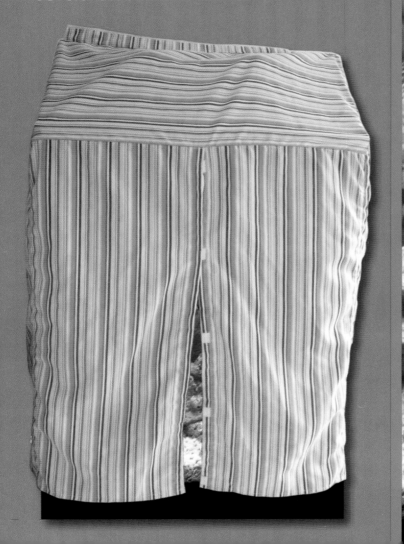

Miss Smith uncovered the big item on her desk. There was an **aquarium** (uh-KWAYR-ee-um). "Yes!" answered Miss Smith. "We have pet fish and this will be their home."

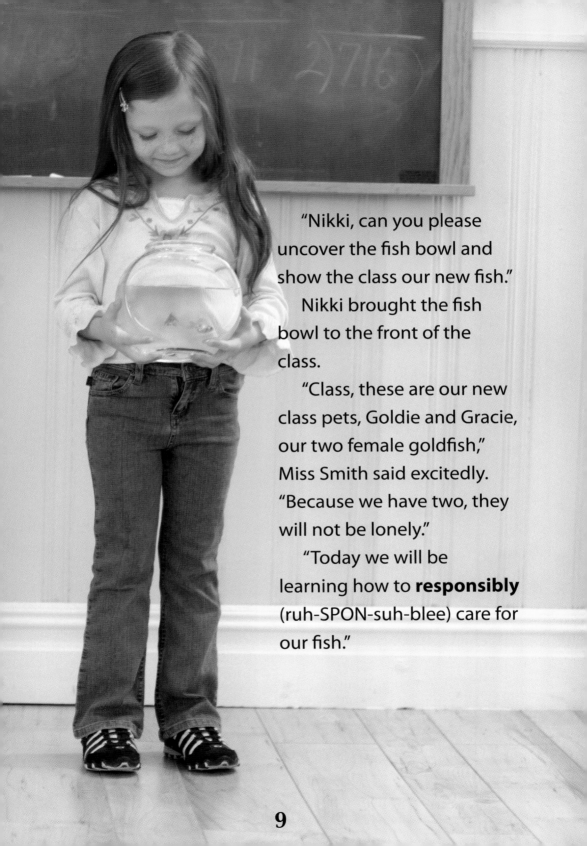

"Nikki, can you please uncover the fish bowl and show the class our new fish."

Nikki brought the fish bowl to the front of the class.

"Class, these are our new class pets, Goldie and Gracie, our two female goldfish," Miss Smith said excitedly. "Because we have two, they will not be lonely."

"Today we will be learning how to **responsibly** (ruh-SPON-suh-blee) care for our fish."

The ranchu is a hooded variety of fancy goldfish from Japan. It is called the "king of goldfish" by the Japanese.

The class gathered around the fish bowl to inspect their new class pets.

"I have goldfish at home!" Malik announced.

"Oh, that's wonderful!" Miss Smith replied. "Would you like to share with the class some tips for how to care for our goldfish here at school?"

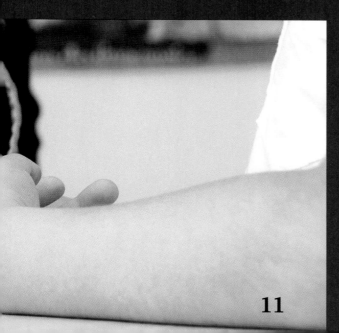

FISH FACT

When choosing more than one goldfish, if you don't want them to breed (make more goldfish), it is best to choose two fish of the same sex. Breeding is a lot of time and work.

11

"Okay," Malik replied. "It's really pretty easy. We will need to feed Goldie and Gracie once a day in the morning. We should give them a small amount of food."

"Who is going to feed them over the weekends?" Shaundra wondered.

"Goldfish can go a few days without being fed. Actually, they can last up to three weeks with no food, but it's not nice to forget about them for that long. Goldie and Gracie will be fine over the weekends while we're at home."

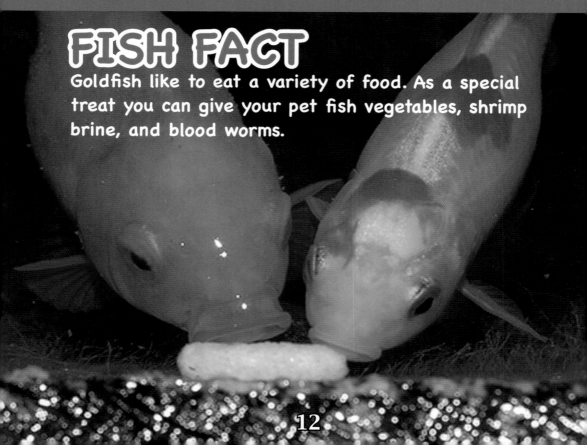

FISH FACT

Goldfish like to eat a variety of food. As a special treat you can give your pet fish vegetables, shrimp brine, and blood worms.

"Do we need to clean the tank?" Anna asked.

"Well," Malik continued, "We might need to use a scrubber to clean out the algae, or the green stuff that will start to grow. We will also need to vacuum the bottom of the tank every few weeks. Someone will need to refill the tank with fresh water when it starts to get low because of **evaporation** (ee-VAH-pur-ay-shun). We will need an adult to help with the cleaning."

"Of course, I will always be available to help with the cleaning of the tank," Miss Smith said.

It is important to test the pH, **ammonia** (uh-MOH-nyuh), **nitrite** (NY-tryte), and **nitrate** (NY-trayt) levels regularly to make sure the water is healthy for your goldfish. The ideal temperature for goldfish is between 20°C (68°F) and 22°C (72°F).

Miss Smith explained to the class, "Goldie and Gracie's new home will be under the bookshelves near the window. They need light, but placing them in front of the window can make them too hot or too cold in the tank.

"I've also included a few decorations and aquarium plants for them, which provide them with food to eat, oxygen to breathe, and shelter to live.

"We will make a poster to put next to their tank so all of you can be reminded of the tools and supplies needed to care for them.

"Like Malik told us earlier, many of the tools need the help of an adult. So let's begin by listing our supplies."

FISH SUPPLIES
1. A small aquarium with pump and filter
2. Fish net scooper
3. Thermometer
4. Gravel for bottom of tank
5. Plants for tank
6. Water testing kit
7. Algae scrubber
8. Decorations
9. Food

"What do you think we can learn from Goldie and Gracie this year, class?" Miss Smith asked the students.

"About how fish live in water," Sara replied.

"The parts of a fish," Alex said.

"The life cycle of a fish," José added.

"You are all correct," Miss Smith answered. "There are many things we can learn from Goldie and Gracie. We will find out how fish breathe, eat, and live by **observing** (ob-ZUR-ving) our new class pet."

FISH FACT

Goldfish can live up to 20+ years if they are fed a varied diet and housed in exceptional (EK-sep-shuh-nul) water conditions. They need to be in tanks that are not overcrowded. They need plenty of swimming room and do best if they are kept with their own breed (kind).

FUN FACT

The longest living goldfish, Tish, lived for 43 years in Thirsk, North Yorkshire, in the United Kingdom. Peter Hand won two goldfish at a fun fair in 1956, Tish and Tosh. Tosh lived until 1975; Tish lived until 1999.

Fish eggs

Adult fish

Fish fry

Young fish

GOLDFISH LIFE CYCLE

Goldfish need a lot of room to swim around. They also need plants so they can hide and lay their eggs.

The female goldfish will lay about 25 eggs, but only the healthy ones will grow up.

The eggs are sticky and attach to the plants.

The male goldfish sprays the eggs so they are **fertilized** (FUR-tih-lyzed) and start to grow baby fish.

The eggs usually hatch in about 3-5 days.

Sometimes the adult goldfish eat the eggs. If you have a fish tank, you should take the adults out so they are away from the eggs.

The eggs soon hatch into fries. A baby goldfish is called a **fry**.

Once they hatch from the eggs the babies (fries) stay attached to the plants for about 2 days.

When the fries start to swim they should be fed fry food.

They gain their adult color after several months.

ANATOMY OF A GOLDFISH

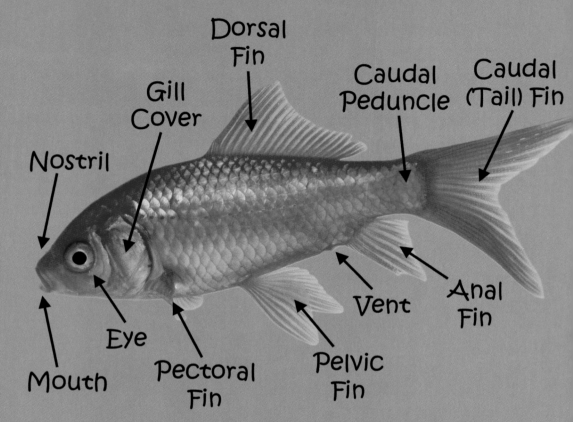

Dorsal Fin

Caudal Peduncle

Caudal (Tail) Fin

Gill Cover

Nostril

Eye

Mouth

Pectoral Fin

Pelvic Fin

Vent

Anal Fin

Anal Fin—A fin that helps to maintain stable balance.
Caudal (CAW-dul) Peduncle (pih-DUN-kul)—The narrow part of a fish's body to which the caudal or tail fin is attached.
Caudal (CAW-dul) Fin—The tail fin of fish used for propulsion (pro-PUHL-shun) during movement.
Dorsal (DOR-sul) Fin—The fin on the back of a fish that helps to maintain balance.
Pectoral (pek-TOH-rul) Fin—Either of two fins, located just behind the head on each side of the fish, that helps to control the direction of movement.
Pelvic (PEL-vik) Fin—A pair of fins attached to the pelvic arch in fish that help control the direction of movement.
Vent—Opening of the digestive tract.

HOW DO FISH BREATHE AND SMELL?

Fish breathe by taking in water through their mouths. Gills on the sides of their heads take the water and get the oxygen from it. Fish do not breathe through their noses like humans do. Fish noses are used to find smells underwater.

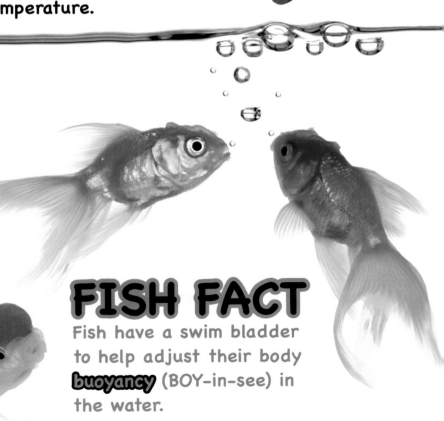

FISH FACT

Goldfish are cold-blooded, so their rate of **metabolism** (muh-TAH-buh-liz-um) depends on water temperature.

FISH FACT

Fish have a swim bladder to help adjust their body **buoyancy** (BOY-in-see) in the water.

23

HOW DO FISH SEE?
Fish have eyes and can see just like we do. One difference between fish eyes and human eyes is that fish eyes do not have lids!

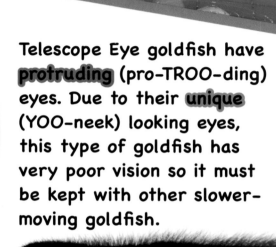

Telescope Eye goldfish have **protruding** (pro-TROO-ding) eyes. Due to their **unique** (YOO-neek) looking eyes, this type of goldfish has very poor vision so it must be kept with other slower-moving goldfish.

Celestial (suh-LESS-chul)
Eye goldfish have eyes
which are turned
upwards, pupils gazing
skyward. When the fry
hatch, the eyes of young
Celestials are normal
but gradually protrude
sideways, and then
turn upwards within a
period of six months.

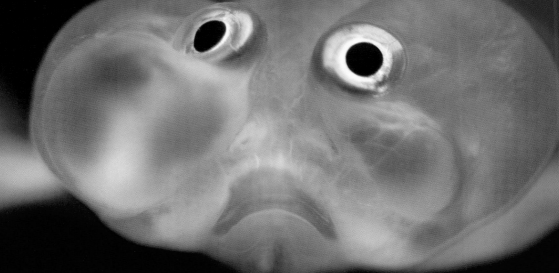

Bubble Eye goldfish have huge fluid-filled sacs with
eyes that point upwards. Their sacs can easily burst
if they swim into pointy objects, so it's best to keep
few decorations in their tanks.

HOW DO FISH HEAR?

Fish do not have ears on the outside of their bodies, but they can hear. Goldfish hear through an inner organ, called an otolith (OH-toh-lyth), which is a hard stone located within the head of the goldfish. If you tap lightly on the tank, the fish might hear it and swim toward you. Don't tap too hard though, or you could frighten the fish.

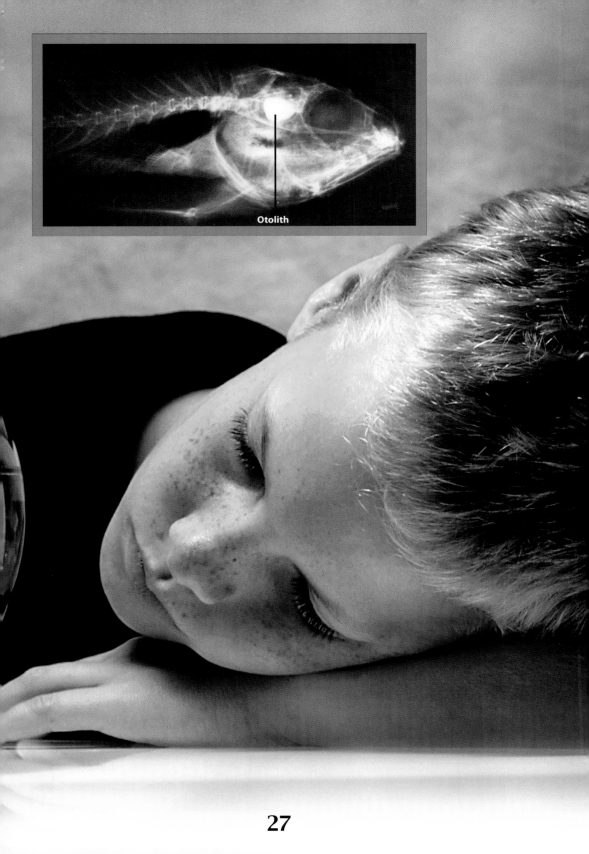

Otolith

DO FISH SLEEP?
Fish sleep just like we do, even without eyelids! Once the tank gets dark, you may notice your fish sinking closer to the bottom of the tank and hiding.

28

COMMON GOLDFISH DISEASES

Goldfish are susceptible (suh-SEP-tuh-bull) to diseases and once they have been infected, it can decrease their life span. The most common reasons goldfish get sick are if the fish tank is dirty, due to poor filtration (fill-TRAY-shun), the water and oxygen levels are too low, the temperatures are either too warm or too cold, and improper feeding. It's important to keep an eye on these things to make sure your goldfish stays healthy. Some common goldfish illnesses are:

Ich (ICK): Body and/or fins are covered with tiny white dots and gills move too quickly. If left untreated, Ich can kill a fish.

Tail or Fin Rot: Fin rot is when a fish's tail or fin looks like it is split or shredded. Sometimes a hole may appear in the middle of the fin.

Fungus: Grey, or grey-white puffs of cottony material covering parts of the fish's body, sometimes covering almost all of the fish's skin. Fungus normally means there is another problem which has weakened the goldfish.

Constipation (kon-STIH-pay-shun): A goldfish is having trouble passing waste and its belly may appear bloated. This is often caused by a diet without enough variety, or by feeding it too many starchy foods.

Dropsy: An infection (in-FEK-shun) that causes a goldfish's scales to stick out from its body.

Swim Bladder Disorder (dys-OR-dur): A goldfish with swim bladder disorder will sometimes float on its side on the water's surface or swim on its side a lot, and its belly may appear bloated.

If you notice your fish acting strangely or any changes in its appearance, consult a veterinarian (veh-truh-NAY-ree-un) for advice and/or treatment.

"Well, class, now that we've learned how to care for Goldie and Gracie, who would like to be this week's helper?" Miss Smith asked.

"I do, I do!" All the students' hands flew into the air. Miss Smith smiled. She knew that Goldie and Gracie would be well taken care of.

A fish should not be left alone during the summer while school is closed, so it will need a nice home to stay in.

FURTHER READING

Books

Bozzo, Linda. *My First Fish*. American Humane Society. Berkeley Heights, NJ: Enslow Publishers Inc., 2008.

Ganeri, Anita. *Goldfish (A Pet's Life)*. Chicago, IL: Heinemann-Raintree, 2nd edition, 2009.

Goodbody, Slim. *Goldfish (Slim Goodbody's Inside Guide to Pets)*. New York, NY: Gareth Stevens Publishing, 2008.

Richardson, Adele. *Caring for Your Fish*. Capstone Press, MN, 2007.

Schuetz, Kari. *Caring for Your Pet Fish*. Pet Care Library. Bellwether Media, Minneaspolis, MN, 2011.

On the Internet

ASPCA
http://www.aspca.org/pet-care/small-pet-care/fish-care.aspx

Best Fish for Kids
http://bestfishforkids.com/tanks.html

Fish Pet Care
http://petcareeducation.com/fish/

Good Goldfish Care
http://www.goodgoldfishcare.com/

How to Take Care of a Goldfish
http://howtotakecareofagoldfish.com/

Most Common Gold Fish Diseases and Treatment
http://ezinearticles.com/?Most-Common-Gold-Fish-Diseases-and-Treatment&id=443179

Pet Fishes Care
http://petfishescare.com/

Pet Goldfish
http://www.petgoldfish.net/

GLOSSARY

ammonia (uh-MOH-nyuh)—A toxic substance that builds up in the aquarium.

aquarium (uh-KWAYR-ee-um)—A tank, bowl, or other water-filled enclosure in which living fish or other aquatic animals and plants are kept.

breed—Members of the same species; to produce offspring.

buoyancy (BOY-in-see)—The ability to float.

disorder (dys-OR-dur)—A sickness that affects the mind of body.

evaporation (ee-VAH-pur-ay-shun)—The disappearing of fluid.

exceptional (EK-sep-shuh-nul)—Well above average.

fertilize (FUR-til-lyze)—When a sperm cell unites with an egg to produce offspring.

filtration (fill-TRAY-shun)—A filtering system that removes waste and other harmful bacteria that builds up in an aquarium.

fry—Small fish, especially young, recently hatched fish.

GLOSSARY

infection (in-FEK-shun)—When a body is affected by germs.
metabolism (muh-TAH-buh-liz-um)—The process by which cells produce the substances and energy needed to sustain life.
nitrate (NY-trayt)—A kind of salt that is poisonous to fish.
nitrite (NY-tryte)—A kind of salt that is poisonous to fish.
observing (ob-ZUR-ving)—Watching and learning from.
protruding (pro-TROO-ding)—Extending out above or beyond.
responsibly (ruh-SPON-suh-blee)—Able to be trusted or depended upon.
susceptible (suh-SEP-tuh-bul)—Likely to be affected.
unique (YOO-neek)—One of a kind.
veterinarian (veh-truh-NAY-ree-un)—An animal doctor.

INDEX

PHOTO CREDITS: pp. 1, 2–3, 4–5, 6–7, 10–11, 16, 17, 21, 23, 24, 25, 26–27, 28–29—Photos.com; pp. 8–9—American Images/Getty Images; pp. 12, 13, 14–15, 19—cc-by-sa; p. 22—Sharon Beck; p. 30—New York Daily News via Getty Images. Every effort has been made to locate all copyright holders of materials used in this book. Any errors or omissions will be corrected in future editions of the book.